PUNK FARM

P. F.

33⅓ RPM · SIDE A

JARRETT J. KROSOCZKA

Alfred A. Knopf

New York

THIS IS A BORZOI BOOK PUBLISHED BY ALFRED A. KNOPF

Copyright © 2005 by Jarrett J. Krosoczka

All rights reserved under International and Pan-American Copyright Conventions. Published in the United States by Alfred A. Knopf, an imprint of Random House Children's Books, a division of Random House, Inc., New York, and simultaneously in Canada by Random House of Canada Limited, Toronto. Distributed by Random House, Inc., New York.

KNOPF, BORZOI BOOKS, and the colophon are registered trademarks of Random House, Inc.

www.randomhouse.com/kids

Library of Congress Cataloging-in-Publication Data

Krosoczka, Jarrett.

Punk Farm / Jarrett J. Krosoczka. — 1st ed.

p. cm.

SUMMARY: At the end of the day, while Farmer Joe gets ready for bed, his animals tune their instruments to perform in a big concert as a rock band called Punk Farm.

ISBN 0-375-82429-4 (trade) — ISBN 0-375-92429-9 (lib. bdg.)

[1. Musicians—Fiction. 2. Rock music—Fiction. 3. Domestic animals—Fiction. 4. Farm life—Fiction.] I. Title.

PZ7.K935Pu 2005

[E]—dc22

2004018803

MANUFACTURED IN CHINA

May 2005

10 9 8 7 6 5 4 3

First Edition

For my brother,
Richard

Farmer Joe works hard all day long.

At the end of the day, Farmer Joe
is tired and heads home for bed.

Farmer Joe's animals are sleepy, too.
But are they getting ready for bed?

Not tonight. They have a show to get ready for.

Cow sets up her drums.

Pig plugs in his amp.

Chicken sets up her keyboards.

Sheep checks the microphone. "Testing . . . 1 . . . 2 . . . 3 . . ."

Goat tunes his bass.

"Okay, gang, tonight's the big night! Let's go over some songs before this place gets packed!"

In the middle of practice, Cow stops drumming.
"Uh . . . guys!" she says. "The farmer's light is on!"

The animals freeze. The microphone screeches.
Footsteps can be heard in the distance.
Will they get caught?

Not tonight. The light goes off, and Punk Farm finishes their rehearsal.

Outside, animals wait in line and buy tickets.
Everyone is eager for the show to start.

"Are you guys ready?" asks Sheep.
"I was born ready," says Pig.
"Whatever, dude," says Goat.

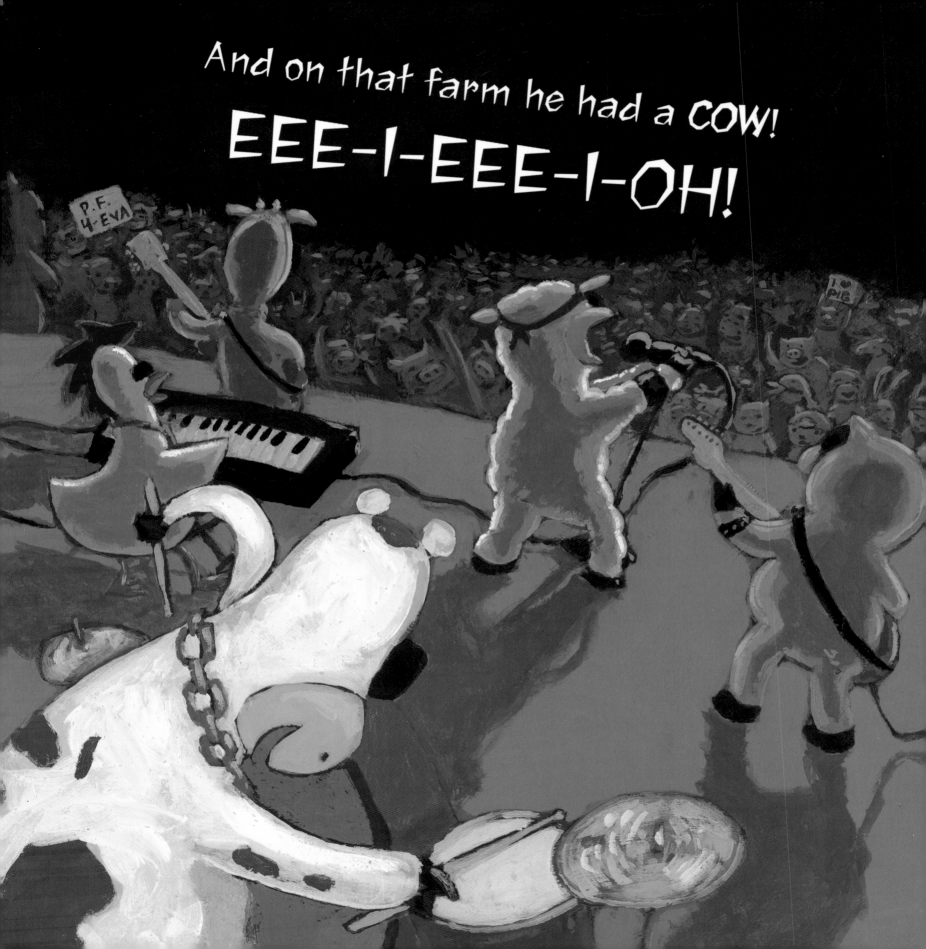

Soon the sun rises and so does Farmer
Joe. He heads over to the barn for . . .

PUNK FARM is:

Sheep - vocals
Pig - guitar
Goat - bass
Chicken - keyboards
Cow - drums